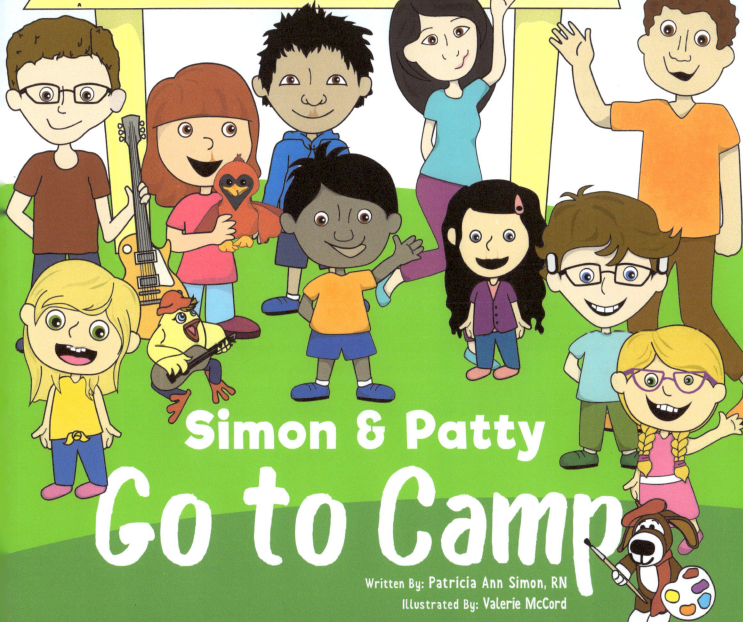

WELCOME

Simon & Patty
Go to Camp

Written By: Patricia Ann Simon, RN

Illustrated By: Valerie McCord

ISBN: 978-0-9988786-6-9
ISBN: 978-0-9988786-7-6

Library of Congress Control Number: 2017905906

When I was 10 years old, my parents signed me up for summer camp. I went to the camp for one day. One day! I was made fun of, laughed at, excluded, and made to feel like I didn't belong.

I felt all alone. I came home from camp and told my parents that I would never go back. Back then, there were no camps for people born with craniofacial differences. There was no camp in which the child, parents and siblings could attend.

Fast forward 40 plus years. When I was in my fifties, I found a camp for individuals affected by facial differences (Children's Craniofacial Association - CCA). This camp is not only for the individual but it is for their siblings and parents. It gives everyone the opportunity to interact with others who have endured similar experiences. This unique weekend retreat allows families to share ideas, problems and solutions, and make life-long friendships. It creates a safe, caring and friendly place where you will be treated with respect. The weekend kicks off with an Educational Symposium and the rest of the weekend allows time and activities to build new relationships and bonds of understanding and caring, which will lend support through both difficult and good times in the future.

This book is dedicated to those children and adults that have felt all alone. Today, you no longer have to feel alone. There are camps out there for you. Camps in which special bonds and positive, life-changing memories can be made. You are not the only special person in the world. There is a community out there extending its hand to you. Please reach out.

WE ARE ALL WONDERS!

FOREWORD

A few years ago, Patricia Simon, wrote and published two beautiful books for children born with facial differences *(Smile with Simon* and *Simon and the Buddy Branch)*. These books became a great success because through simple stories, they introduced the interactions and feelings of children born with facial differences to the rest of their peers. These books were also indirectly addressed to parents, educators and the public in general and brought a powerful message: there are among us people born with facial differences who should not be marginalized. They deserve our acceptance, respect and love as any other person.

Ms. Simon recently expanded her work with two additional books: *Simon and Patty Go To Camp* and *Simon and the Bully.*

Unfortunately, bullying among children and adults is real in our society and every effort to eradicate it is welcome. Children can be very cruel to their peers and these books, in a simplistic but powerful way, brings the message of tolerance and acceptance of all human beings regardless of their different appearances. "So let's all be kind to one another," should become the motto of all children, parents and teachers in an effort to improve our society and interactions with each other!

In *Simon and Patty Go To Camp,* the theme of facial differences is repeated, but here children affected with differences are encouraged to express their feelings, avoid self-isolation, not to be shy and above all, to understand that they are special and that "beyond the face there is a heart." There is advice for "normal" people as well: Accept these kids for who they are and that regardless of appearance, we are all the same. Each person deserves to be treated with friendliness, compassion, kindness and, of course, love.

What a beautiful gift Patricia Simon is giving us!

I wish these books become mandatory reading for all children and adults and especially, teachers. Imagine their impact on the new generation through promotion of respect for all, improvement of self-esteem regardless of appearance and above all, reduction of bullying which could have significant and long lasting effects on the growing children.

Once again, thank you Pat very much for these incredible initiatives.

Mimis Cohen MD, FACS, FAAP
Professor and Chief Division of
Plastic, Reconstruction and Cosmetic Surgery
University of Illinois, Chicago
Director Craniofacial Center UIC

Patty and her little sister, Abigail nervously sat in the back seat. They were excited their friend Simon could join them for this new adventure.

"So, are you all excited about camp?" Mom asked.

"I'm excited, I've never been to camp before," Abigail said.
"I'm excited to meet new friends," Simon chirped.
"I'm really scared," Patty answered. "The last time I went to camp, everyone made fun of me and wouldn't play with me. I'll never forget how awful I felt."

Mom smiled as they pulled into the entrance of the camp.
**"Everyone is accepted for who they are, here.
Isn't that wonderful?** This will be a weekend
for making new memories and friends.
Next stop, camp registration!"

Patty and her family waited in line until it was their turn.
"My name is Erica," a counselor said. **"Welcome to camp.**
We're all so excited you are here. It's going to be a super fun weekend."
Annie, another counselor, handed Mom the agenda.

"You're just in time.
Everyone is gathering for the
camp kick-off.
See you there!"

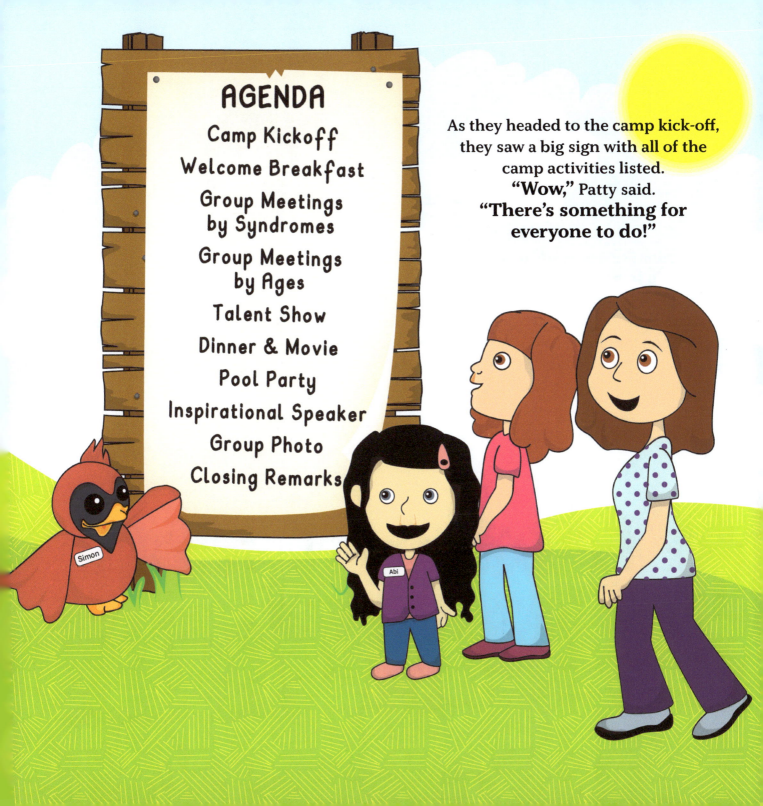

AGENDA

Camp Kickoff

Welcome Breakfast

Group Meetings by Syndromes

Group Meetings by Ages

Talent Show

Dinner & Movie

Pool Party

Inspirational Speaker

Group Photo

Closing Remarks

As they headed to the camp kick-off, they saw a big sign with all of the camp activities listed. **"Wow,"** Patty said. **"There's something for everyone to do!"**

WE ARE WONDERS

Beyond The Face Is A Heart

CHOOSE TO BE HAPPY!

Counselor Erica welcomed everyone at the kick-off. **"This is a safe place where you can be yourself, and people can understand.** Most importantly, you will develop lasting friendships based on kindness, compassion and love for one another. We are a wonderful, supportive community, and we're so happy you are here with us!"

After the camp kick-off,
a girl walked over to Patty and Abigail.
**"Hi, my name is Mariana,
but you can call me Mari."**
"Hi, I'm Abigail, but you can call me Abi." Both girls
giggled. And, this is my big sister Patty.

Patty shyly said, "This is our first time coming to a
camp like this, so we don't know anyone."

**"Well, now you
know me,"** Mari said with
a giggle. **"Do you want
to play hula hoops with
me and my friends?"**

"Sure," Patty replied,
"but first we need to tell our
mom where we are.
Let's meet back here in a few
minutes!" Patty and Abi
then ran to tell their Mom
about their new friend.

AGENDA

Camp Kickoff

Welcome Breakfast

Group Meetings
by Syndromes

Group Meetings
by Ages

Talent Show

Dinner & Movie

Pool Party

Inspirational Speaker

Group Photo

Closing Remarks

While the girls played, Simon went searching for friends.

As he flew, he was excited to hear music. Simon loved to chirp to his favorite songs, so he followed the music to an older dog painting and a chick playing the guitar. **"Hi, my name is Simon. You play very well."**

"Thanks! My name is Chick Jagger and this is my friend, Picasso."

"So nice to meet you both," Simon said. **"I've never been to a camp before, but this looks like fun."**

"I come every year," said Picasso. "Hey, do you want to check out the hotel lobby with us?" Simon nodded his head and off they went.

Peter was also on his way to meet his friend Mari
at the hotel, when he came across a boy sitting alone.

"Hi, I'm Peter," he said to
the lonely boy. "What's your name?"

"Matthew," the boy shyly replied.

"Can I sit with you and tune my guitar?"

"Sure," the boy softly replied.

"I like playing the guitar," Peter said.
"What do you like to do?"

The boy smiled. "I'm really good
at sports. My favorite team is
the Chicago Cubs."

Later in the day, everyone went to the **pool party.** There was swimming, and beach balls, and games. **Something for everyone!**

All the campers sat together and talked about tomorrow night's talent show.

"Hey guys," Peter asked, "are you going to perform at the talent show?"
Everyone shook their heads. "NO!"
"Come on, it will be fun," said Peter.
"I don't want to go up there by myself," Matthew replied.
"Me neither," said Mari.
"How about we write a song?" Patty suggested.
"Then we can sing it at the talent show."
The campers cheered. **"Yes, let's do it together!"**

The kids rehearsed their song for the talent show.
Peter and Chick Jagger played guitar.
Abi played the maracas and Picasso played the sticks.
Simon chirped as all the campers sang along.

It was almost time for the inspirational speaker gathering.
Mari was going to give her first talk ever!

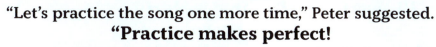

"Let's practice the song one more time," Peter suggested.
"Practice makes perfect!
Then we can all go listen to Mari's talk!"
"Great idea," said Patty.

Finally, it was time for the inspirational talk.
Mari smiled at the other campers and began.

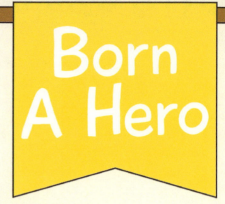

**"Hi, everyone. My name is Mari
and I was born a hero.**
I have Pfeiffer Syndrome. My body tells my bones to
grow differently. It was just the way I was born.

My bones grow before they are supposed to, and extra
bones can grow anywhere in my body. I can't really do
anything about it. That's my story!

I'm very smart and want to be a doctor one day.
Oh, and I must say, I have the cutest
big toes in the room!"

Born A Hero

"My words of wisdom to you are: **don't worry about what others think. Stand up and stand out.** Let's be the example! **Let's accept people for who they are,** love others, and reach out to new members in our community. See, I told you I was smart." Mari giggled and the crowd couldn't help smiling back.

"Let me end by saying, **let's widen the circle** of acceptance for individuals with facial differences!"

After her speech, Mari asked, "What did you guys learn?"

"I learned I can do anything I want to do," Patty said.
"Nothing can hold me back."

"We are all rock stars!" Peter added.

"Everyone is different and that's what make us great!"
Matthew said, and Abi told them **she didn't feel alone anymore.**

"I'm so happy,"
Mari told her friends.

While the adults talked, the kids had a surprise outside play time!

All the children
picked their favorite
outdoor activities.

Chick Jagger, Picasso,
and Simon joined
in the fun too!

"Hey everybody, the talent show is tomorrow," Peter reminded everyone. "How about one last practice before dinner?"

"Yes, let's practice!" Mari said. "I have an idea for some dance moves. We can practice them at the dance tonight."

After dinner, the campers put on glow-in-the-dark necklaces and bracelets. **They danced, and sang, and laughed** until the camp counselors said, "Last song of the night. You all have to go to bed soon. The talent show is tomorrow after breakfast."

Everyone practiced hard the next morning before the talent show.
"I'm so nervous," Matthew said as he jumped up and down.
"It's almost time to perform our song."

"Oh no!" Peter shouted. "I forgot my ear."
"Your ear?" asked Abi.

"Yes, I have a prosthetic ear," replied
Peter. "I need to run upstairs and put it on. I'll
be right back, and then we'll be ready to go!"
"After the talent show, I'll show you how my
prosthetic ear snaps on and off.
It's really cool," Peter told Abi.

Finally, it was time for the talent show.
This year's theme was **We Got Talent.**
Matthew and Patty walked quietly to the microphone.

**"We wrote this song to sing to you.
It's called, We are Wonders."**

"**Judge less while we love more,**" they sang together. "Spread the message within shore to shore. Open minds will open arms!

We are wonders. Yes, we are all wonders. It's true!"

When they finished singing, everyone in the audience stood and applauded.

Come on. We are going to be late for the group photo. **We need to all be wearing our camp T-shirt!**

Group Photo

Erica and Annie, the camp counselors,
told everyone to gather together for the
annual camp group photo.

LOVE MORE JUDGE LESS

You Are A SUPERHERO

EXTEND YOUR HAND T OTHERS

After the group photo, everyone gathered for the counselor's closing speech.

"Thank you to our camp sponsors and volunteers," Counselor Erica began. "This was, yet again, a wonderful weekend in which new friendships were made and old ones were strengthened. Look around. **This is unconditional love!** Imagine a world where all people are accepted for who they are, not how they look. Let's continue to treat people with respect. **We are a community, and we're here for you—always!"**

All too soon, it was time for the campers to head home.

Picasso and Chick Jagger
happily replied,
**"Smile with Simon
and be kind!"**

Simon said to Picasso and Chick
Jagger, **"It was so cool being
able to hang out with you guys
this weekend.** I had a blast and
can't wait to tell my bird friends.
Remember what I taught you?"

As they drove home, Patty fell asleep with a smile on her face. She dreamed of the world the counselors spoke of, where everyone was accepted for who they are, not how they look.

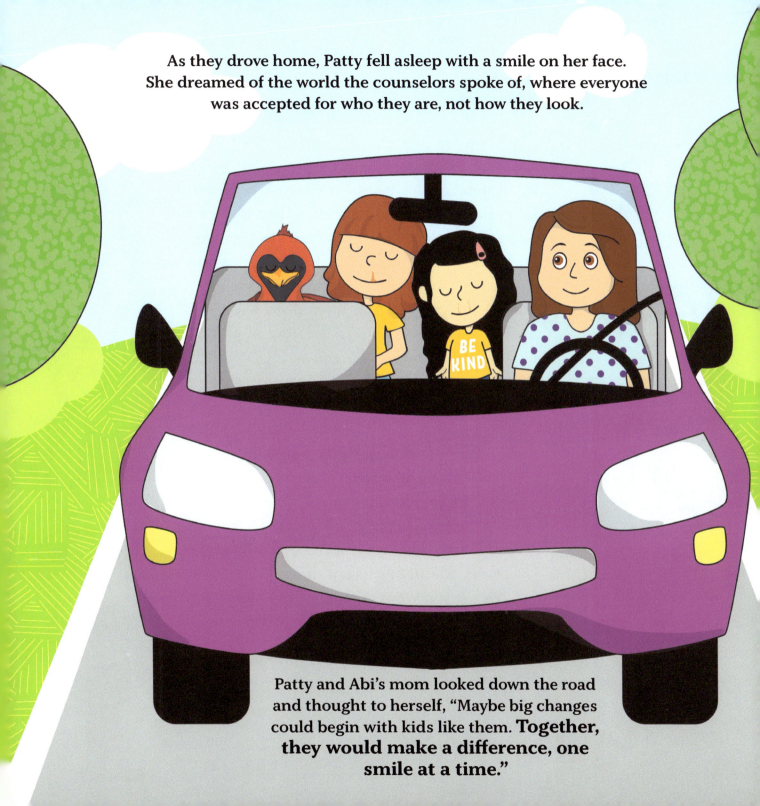

Patty and Abi's mom looked down the road and thought to herself, "Maybe big changes could begin with kids like them. **Together, they would make a difference, one smile at a time.**"

We Are Wonders

We all stand up tall. Want our voices to be heard
We know that understanding is more than just a word
Walk a mile in our shoes, a few hours in our heart
My eyes are your eyes. There's beauty in this art
I can root for you and you can root for me
Together's always better. Try and you will see

Judge less. Love more
Spread the message within and shore to shore
Open minds will open arms

We we are wonders, yes we are all wonders
We are all wonders it's true
We we are wonders, yes we are all wonders
We are all wonders that's right
We'll watch each other grow and accept who we are
Every one among us is a shining star
We get you What a wonder-full thing
Always and forever that's what we bring
We are all beautiful, beautiful

Smile
with Simon

We may not be the same
And if we were it'd be a shame
You have a voice let go and sing
Open up just spread your wings
You've got to feel good about yourself
You've got to feel good about yourself

I am different but I am beautiful
We are different but we are beautiful
We're still alike in many ways

Cardinals, sparrows and blue jays
We fall sometimes but that's okay
Pick yourself up and seize the day

So smile with Simon and be kind
Smile and see what you will find
So smile with Simon this is his song
His badge of courage makes him strong

We are different but we are beautiful
Simon can lift you up my friend
So come fly and watch as we ascend
True friends are out there you will see
Lean on them in times of need

So smile with Simon and be kind
Smile and see what you will find
So smile with Simon this is his song
His badge of courage makes him strong

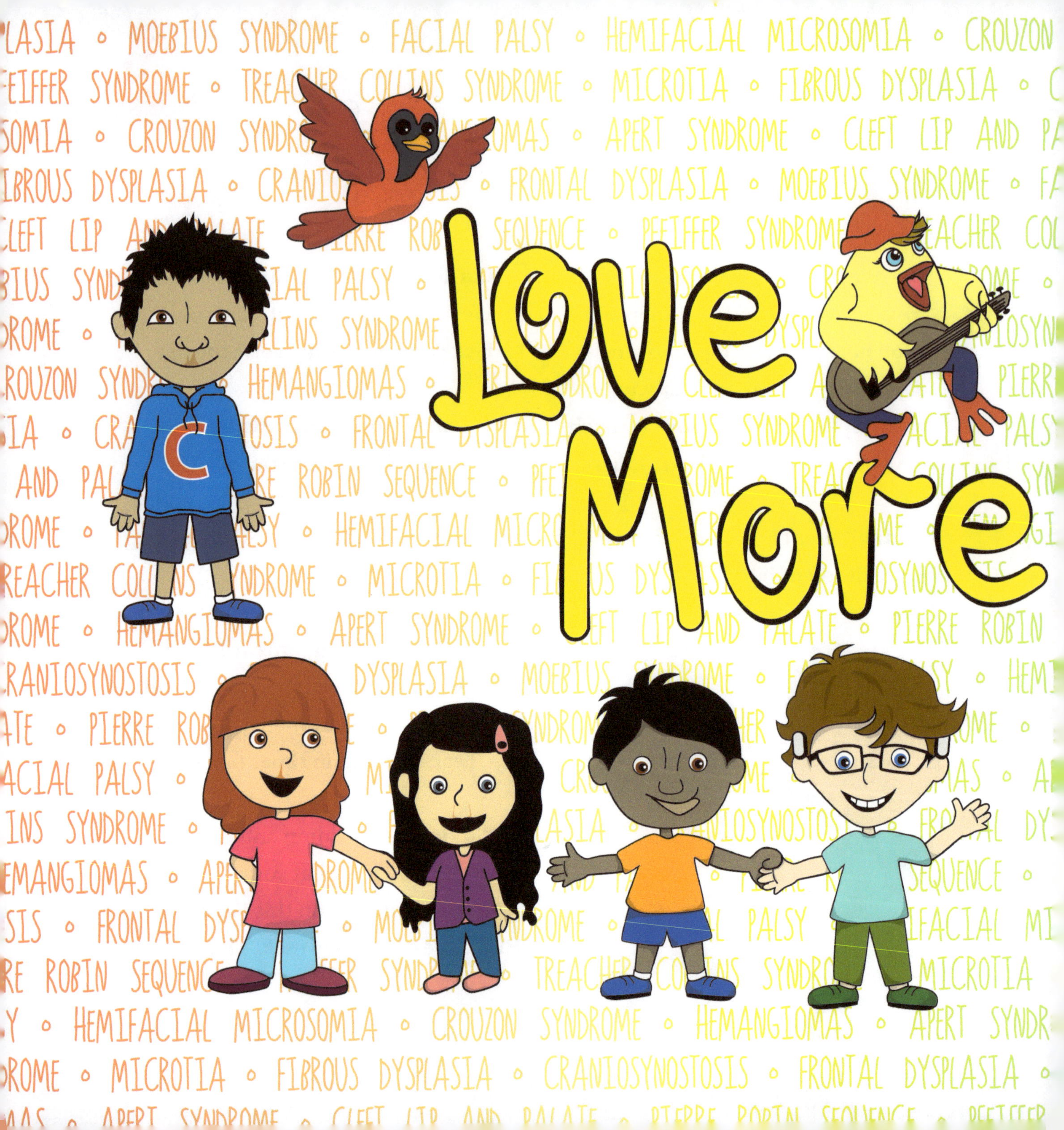
Love More

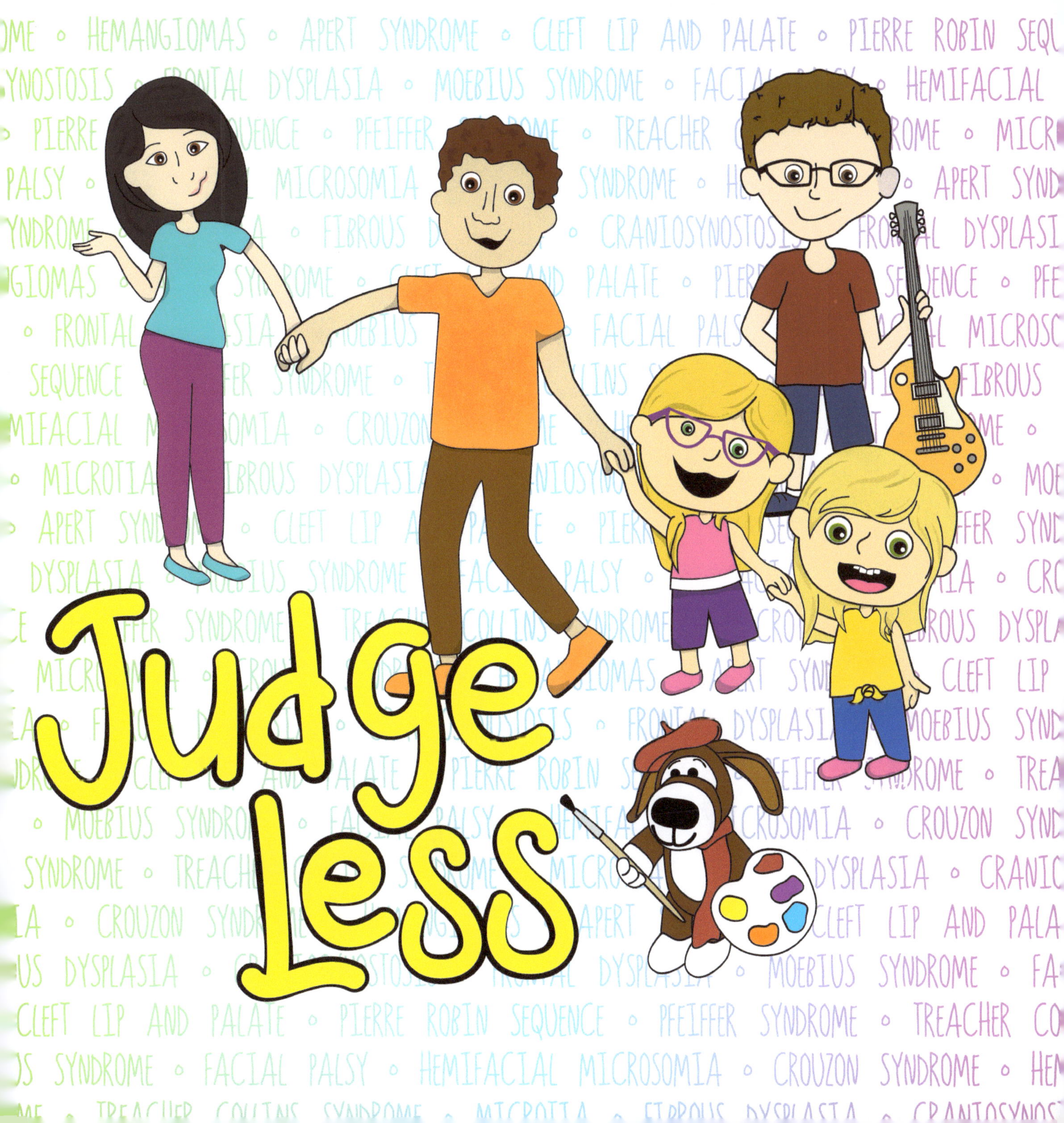
Judge
Less

WE ARE WONDERS

JUDGE LESS
LOVE MORE

SIMON'S FAVORITES

AboutFace.ca
ACPA American Cleft Palate-Craniofacial Association
Bear Necessities Pediatric Cancer Foundation
Beauty with a Twist
BORN A HERO, Pfeiffer's Health and Social Issues Awareness
Camp About Face
Cary Kanno-Musical Artist
Children's Craniofacial Association (CCA Kids)
CleftProud
Cuddles For Clefts
Doctors Without Borders
Emory Cleft Project-Dept Human Genetics, Emory Univ School of Medicine
Face the Future Foundation Illinois
FACES: The National Craniofacial Association
Facing Forward Inc
Love Me Love My Face: Jono Lancaster
MyFace
National Organization for Rare Disorders (NORD)
Noordhoff Craniofacial Foundation Philippines, Inc
Operation of Hope Worldwide
Operation Smile
Patients Rising
Pete's Diary: Peter Dankelson. Motivational Speaker
Rare Disease Legislative Advocates (RDLA)
Joe Rutland -CleftThoughts
Smile Train
Solidarity Bridge.org
St. Jude Children's Research Hospital
UI Health Craniofacial Center at the UIC College of Medicine

ABOUT PATRICIA ANN SIMON

I am a RN and was born with a cleft lip and palate.

I have written four books, *Smile with Simon, Simon and the Buddy Branch, Simon and Patty Go To Camp,* and *Simon and the Bully.* These children's books resonate with young people suffering from similar craniofacial differences.

My first children's book, *Smile with Simon* is about a cardinal named Simon, who's born with a gap in his beak. His gap made it difficult for him to eat, smile, and sing. In the story, he meets a young girl named Patty, who relates with Simon because she has a cleft lip.

I wrote a second book, *Simon and the Buddy Branch,* which further stresses the importance of kindness, love, and acceptance in the lives of children with facial differences.

My aim is to help children born with facial differences understand that it's okay to be different. I want to remind them that they are beautiful.

I am also a member of American Cleft Palate-Craniofacial Association (ACPA), Children's Craniofacial Association (CCA), Cleft Community Advisory Council (CCAC) for Smile Train, and former board member of Face the Future Foundation, which supports the efforts of University of Illinois Health Craniofacial Center.

I have given a keynote speech for the Inaugural Cleft Lip and Palate Team Day at Morgan Stanley Children's Hospital in New York Presbyterian Hospital,

My book, *Smile with Simon* was translated to Tagalog so that it could be used at a Philippine speech camp.

I created a webpage, www.smilewithsimon.org which features videos and songs that reinforce the message we are all different, and to be accepting and kind.

Books can be purchased directly through my website:
www.smilewithsimon.org

CPSIA information can be obtained
at www.ICGtesting.com
Printed in the USA
LVHW070711280921
698836LV00008B/79